W9-ARY-255

Sophie Makes a Splash

The Mermaid S.O.S. series

Sophie Makes a Splash

gillian shields

illustrated by helen turner

BLOOMSBURY
CHILDREN'S
BOOKS

Map o

Coral Kingdom

Cauldron
Clif

First published in Great Britain in 2006 by Bloomsbury Publishing Plc.
Published in the United States in 2008 by Bloomsbury U.S.A. Children's Books
175 Fifth Avenue, New York, New York 10010
Distributed to the trade by Macmillan

Library of Congress Cataloging-in-Publication Data available upon request
ISBN-13: 978-1-59990-212-8 • ISBN-10: 1-59990-212-5

First U.S. Edition 2008
Printed in the U.S.A. by Quebecor World Fairfield
2 4 6 8 10 9 7 5 3 1

All papers used by Bloomsbury U.S.A. are natural, recyclable products
made from wood grown in well-managed forests. The manufacturing
processes conform to the environmental regulations of the country of origin.

For Sophie
—G. S.

This book is for my truly
fantastic friends who make
sure life is never dull!

Love —H. T.

Prologue

Meet Misty, Ellie, Sophie, Holly, Lucy, and Scarlett. They are Mermaid Sisters of the Sea, who live in the magical underwater world of Coral Kingdom. The Merfolk and their wise ruler, Queen Neptuna, look after the sea and all its creatures.

Coral Kingdom is protected by six powerful magic crystals, which give life and strength to the Merfolk.

Without the crystals, Coral Kingdom would not survive.

Every year, the old crystals fade and have to be replaced. Queen Neptuna sends Misty and her friends—six special mermaids who are pure of heart—to collect the new ones from the secret Crystal Cave. But as they are bringing the crystals home, a storm blows the mermaids completely off course.

This is no ordinary storm! It is created by Mantora, Queen Neptuna's jealous sister. Mantora wanted to rule Coral Kingdom, and now she is bitter and full of hatred. She is determined to stop the mermaids from returning home, so that she can overthrow Queen Neptuna and set up her evil Storm Kingdom instead.

Luckily, the young mermaids have courage and friendship on their side. But that's not all; their S.O.S. Kits will help them as they race to get the crystals back safely. And they never forget their Mermaid Pledge:

We promise that we'll take good care
Of all sea creatures everywhere.
We'll never hurt and never break,
We'll always give and never take.
And as we fight Mantora's threat,
This saying we must not forget:
"I'll help you and you'll help me,
For we are Sisters of the Sea!"

Sophie and her friends are
eager to prove that Queen Neptuna
was right to trust them with the
precious crystals. They are going
to do everything it takes to get
them home and safeguard Coral
Kingdom for another year.

Will Mantora win? Or can the
mermaids get the new crystals back
in time to stop the light fading
forever from Coral Kingdom?

Sophie

Chapter One

"Good-bye! Good-bye!" called the mermaids Sophie, Misty, Ellie, Holly, Lucy, and Scarlett. They were looking up from the sparkling sea, waving farewell to the great albatross. "And thank you!"

The king of the birds called his own wild farewell. He and his folk were returning to their rocky island home, where earlier that day the mermaids had rescued some white terns from a very sticky situation. The albatross and his brothers wheeled away, bearing giant clam shells that hung from ropes of twisted seaweed. A moonlight ride in these pearly carriages had helped the mermaids on their way after their kind deed. As they looked up, they saw the stately birds swoop into the path of the sunrise.

"Thank you so much," Sophie called one last time. Then she turned to the others bobbing up and down in the water. "It's time for us to swim west to Coral Kingdom!"

The brave young friends were the Crystal Keepers for Queen Neptuna. They had to deliver six glittering new crystals to her by the end of the week, or the power of Coral Kingdom would fade forever.

"I wish we could fly all the way home," sighed Ellie, as they checked that their crystals were safe in the pouches tied around their waists.

"Being carried through the air in the shells really was like flying," said Sophie, fastening the belt of her pouch tightly, "but I'm glad to be back in the sea again. This is where mermaids belong!"

She did a spectacular somersault and dived under the waves as gracefully as a dolphin. Then she burst through the water again, shaking diamond drops of water from her fun, spiky hair. Her gleaming orange tail swirled in the clear waves like a bright ribbon.

"You don't have to show off and make a splash, Sophie," grumbled Scarlett. "We're just as ready for a good swim as you are."

They all felt refreshed and lively after their sleep. But there was still a long way to go on their journey, with perhaps new dangers to face.

"I hope Mantora isn't planning anything to try and stop us," said Lucy anxiously. "All the difficulties we've met seem to have been caused by her. She's determined that we won't get the crystals home in time."

"We'll have to keep a careful watch for any sign of her," agreed Misty. She looked to see if the frayed ends of her belt were tied together firmly. Misty had almost lost her crystal a few days ago, so she had to make absolutely sure that it couldn't happen again. Next time she might not get it back. "I'm ready now," she declared. "Should we swim deep under the sea? That way any humans out early in their fishing boats won't see us."

"Good idea," said Sophie. "Let's go!"

One by one the friends arched high in the air, before plunging down in a swift dive. Their mermaid tails glinted like jewels in the sunlight—orange, pink, red, yellow, purple, and green. Then only a splash of white foam was left behind, and the mermaids were gone, hidden under the waves.

Underwater was like a different world, thought Sophie. The morning sun shone through the sea and made everything glow. Golden specks of sand glittered in the water when the mermaids swished their tails. They dived farther into the cool, mysterious depths. The distant sound of dolphins calling to each other echoed all around.

"Isn't the sea beautiful?" said Sophie, as the mermaids swam side by side in perfect harmony. A shoal of young tuna fish darted past. Tiny silvery bubbles streamed up from the seabed below. "And there are so many different creatures and oceans to get to know!"

"If only the humans could see this," murmured Lucy. "Then they would fight with us against Mantora and everything

that harms the sea. I want to help its creatures to be safe forever."

"The best way we can do that is to get the crystals home in time," said Scarlett crisply. "Why don't we swim a little faster instead of admiring the scenery?"

"All right, Scarlett," said Ellie. "If you want to go faster, what about having a swimming race?"

"But Sophie will win easily!" laughed Misty. "She's definitely the best swimmer of all of us."

Scarlett looked a little bit annoyed. She thought that she was just as good of a swimmer as Sophie.

"How do you know?" she said sulkily. "Sophie can't win every race. She might not win this one."

Sophie wasn't worried about that, though. She loved to swim fast, but she knew there were more important things than winning all the time.

"I don't mind who wins," she said good-naturedly. "Ellie's right, a race will make us swim faster and get the crystals home sooner. Let's line up for the start!"

The young mermaids all swirled their tails quickly and came to a stop. Then they stretched out their arms and held hands, until they were in a perfect starting line. A drowsy shark, slowly drifting home to rest after a busy night, looked up and saw them.

"What foolish young things," she

tut-tutted. "They should be hiding under a rock. Don't they know that Mantora has been charging around these waters, looking for trouble? Maybe I should go and warn them."

She sleepily waved a fin to catch the attention of the mermaids. But they were too busy getting ready for the race to notice.

"Coral Kingdom lies straight ahead," Sophie said to the others. "Are you all ready?"

"We're ready," they called excitedly.

"Then one, two, three, GO!" said Sophie. The race was on!

Chapter Two

Sophie soon surged away in front of the others, her fiery orange tail rippling powerfully through the water. She really was a fast, sleek swimmer. Scarlett charged forward, determined to catch up with her. Then Misty quickly shot ahead to be tied with Scarlett. After a sudden burst of speed, Holly caught up with both of them. Compared to the others, Lucy wasn't such a strong swimmer. She preferred to swim calmly and steadily, so she was soon left behind.

"Hold my hand, Lucy," said Ellie, going back to keep her company. "We'll swim together. Let's see if we can catch them!"

All the mermaids enjoyed racing through the sparkling sea. It felt good to know that

they were getting the crystals closer to
home. They sang joyously as they swam:

Faster, faster through the sea!
Who is quicker—you or me?
Faster, faster we must go,
Ever onward, swift not slow!

The friends swept along determinedly, their long hair streamed out like silk—golden, red, soft brown, and raven black. Some shiny-shelled lobsters looked up from the sandy seabed to admire them.

"Marvelous swimmers, those mermaids!" they exclaimed, waving their sharp pincers. "They look like they want to get somewhere quickly. Wonder what they're in such a hurry about."

Sophie and her friends hoped that they had shaken Mantora off their trail at last. They surged toward the western seas, where Coral Kingdom lay hidden from human eyes in the far distance. Sophie was ahead in the race, but Scarlett was quickly catching up with Sophie's vivid orange tail.

"I'm nearly tied with you," Scarlett called triumphantly.

Sophie laughed and sprinted forward. But then she swam straight into something that was invisibly blocking the way.

"OUCH!" she cried, stopping so suddenly that Scarlett crashed into her. Then Misty collided with Scarlett. Soon all the mermaids bumped into each other in a confused heap.

"OW! Ouch! What happened?" the friends exclaimed, as they rubbed their stinging arms.

"Oh, my poor head!" said Ellie.

"And my tail!" said Sophie. Then they all looked up to see what had forced them to stop.

In front of them was a loosely woven

net. It was made from ropes the same pale color as the water, so it was difficult to see. The holes in the net were too small for a mermaid to swim through.

"So that's what we bumped into," said Sophie wonderingly. "An invisible wall of net."

It waved silently and menacingly in the current, like a giant spider's web.

"Be careful, everyone," called Holly. "Stay away from it. This might be dangerous."

"It's a little spooky," said Lucy nervously. "Do you think it has something to do with Mantora?"

"I don't know," replied Misty, as the mermaids hovered in the water, gazing at

the huge barrier. "But we'll have to get past it somehow. I just wish it wasn't so big!"

The strange net really was enormous. It reached all the way from the seabed below, up to the surface of the water above the mermaids' heads. From side to side it sliced through the water like an endless brick wall. The mermaids quickly took

out their radiant crystals and shone
them over the huge expanse so they could
see it better.

"Do you know what I think?" said
Holly, as she examined it from a cautious
distance. "I think it's a fishing net."

Sophie and the others listened to Holly
carefully. She was very smart and knew
about all sorts of things.

"But isn't it too big for that?" Ellie asked.

"This kind of net is big," said Holly.
"Ordinary fishing nets are like sacks that
scoop up the catch. But
this one is called a
gill net. My dad
told me about
them. They stretch
through the water

like a wall. When a plump fish tries to swim through one of the holes, his gills and fins get caught. Then he can't swim forward or backward to free himself."

"Poor things," said Lucy sadly. "How awful to be trapped in a net."

"I know, Lucy," said Misty, "but it is Mother Nature's way. All the creatures need to find their food, even humans."

"But do the humans really need to catch *so many* fish?" asked Ellie. "This net will hold thousands of fish when it is full."

"I'm afraid the humans can be just as greedy as Mantora," said Holly wisely. "In the old days, the fisher folk only took enough from the sea to feed themselves and their families. But now these big new gill nets catch everything they can."

41

"Even mermaids," shivered Lucy. "I'm glad I'm not caught in it."

"Can't we just swim to the surface and leap over the top of it up there?" asked Sophie. The others thought this was a sensible idea, but Holly stopped them.

"No!" she said. "There might be humans waiting in their fishing boats on the surface to haul in their catch later on. We shouldn't go near them!"

"Then we'll have to swim along until we find an opening," said Sophie. "It's a shame to be delayed just now. We were moving so quickly."

"And I was nearly beating you," added Scarlett.

"We'll have to finish the race another time," replied Sophie, with a quick smile.

"That doesn't matter now—we've got to find a way to get around this net!"

The mermaids turned to their left and followed the line of the webbed ropes, holding their glimmering crystals high to clearly light the way. They were searching for an opening big enough to slip through, so they could continue their journey. The friends were all impatient to get home to Coral Kingdom.

"Is this awful gill net going to go on forever?" complained Scarlett, as they swam along. The other mermaids started to look worried too. The wall of net bent away ahead of them until they couldn't see where it ended. But just then they heard something that sent a shiver down their spines.

"H-e-e-e-lp!"

"What's that?" asked Misty.

The sad, wailing cry echoed through the water again. It seemed to come from in front of the mermaids.

"Help! Ple-e-e-ase help!"

"Someone's in trouble," said Sophie. "We've got to find them!"

The mermaids surged forward anxiously. As they swam around the curving wall of the huge net, a little gray shape came rushing toward them.

"Oh!" exclaimed the friends in surprise.

It was an adorable baby dolphin, with soft flippers and big, dark eyes. And the mermaids could see that he looked as though his heart might break.

Chapter Three

"Please come quickly," he sobbed.

"What's the matter, little one?" said Sophie kindly, as she put her twinkling crystal away.

"It's my . . . it's my . . . ," the baby dolphin gulped. He was crying so hard that he could barely speak.

"It's your what?" smiled Misty.

"It's my mommy," he wailed. "She's caught in the nasty net."

The mermaids looked at the sobbing young creature with concerned faces. This sounded like a job for the Sisters of the Sea!

"Can you show us where she is?" asked Scarlett. "As fast as you can?"

"She's over here," he sniffed. "And she's hurt!"

He dashed away, and the mermaids swiftly followed him. Soon, they could see where the big gill net came to an end in the distance. But some way before that, the mermaids saw the streamlined shape of a dolphin. She was stuck in a wide gash in the net, tangled in its twisted, trailing ropes. The frantic mother was rolling from side to side, lashing her tail and trying to escape.

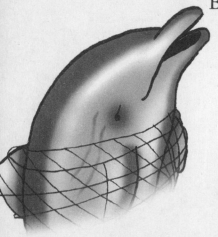 But each move pinned her even more tightly in the knotted web.

"Mommy!" the little dolphin cried. He laid his snuffly beak on her face. "I

found some sparkly fish to
help you."

"Good boy, Smudge,"
panted his mother
weakly. She looked at
Sophie and her friends.
"Ah, you are mermaids!
My name is Silver. You
can see that I'm trapped!"

"How did this happen?" asked Sophie
urgently.

"We were traveling with my sisters and
their young," Silver replied faintly, "on our
way to the Wild Waves. My son suddenly
heard a strange noise, as though someone was
calling him, so he darted after the sound."

"I didn't know it was a bad thing to
do," wept Smudge. "I'm sorry."

"I followed him," continued his mother with an effort. "We saw this huge net ahead of us. A hole had been torn in it, maybe by a boat. Smudge slipped through, and I tried to follow but got stuck!"

"What were you swimming toward, Smudge?" asked Ellie gently.

"There was someone calling me," said Smudge. "When I swam through the hole in the net, I saw her. She had a tail like yours, but she was scary looking. I didn't like her, so I turned around and swam back here to my mommy."

"That sounds like Mantora!" exclaimed Lucy.

"I fear that it was," gasped the mother dolphin.

"Don't worry, Silver, we'll set you free,"

said Sophie. The friends eagerly tried to undo the twisted ropes. But they were in tight knots around Silver. The shiny, slippery netting was too hard for mermaid fingers to untie. At last, Sophie and her friends had to admit defeat.

"I think we'll need to get some help," said Misty. "There's nothing in our S.O.S. Kits that could cut through this hard, human-made rope. We'll go and see what we can find, then come back."

Misty was about to dash away when Holly called out, "Wait! It's not that simple."

Silver raised her head feebly.

"Yes," she whispered, "I cannot wait for you to get help. If I don't swim to the surface very soon to breathe, I will not survive."

Misty, Ellie, Lucy, and Scarlett looked shocked.

"You see," Sophie explained, "dolphins aren't like us. They can't just swim underwater for as long as they like."

"They have to keep going up to the surface to breathe in air through their blowhole," added Holly.

"My mommy can't breathe!" cried Smudge. He nuzzled against her unhappily.

"But we're going to help her to breathe," said Sophie in a clear, calm voice. "We're going to think of something, Smudge. And we're going to think of it quickly!"

Lucy cuddled Smudge, and Ellie soothed Silver by stroking her smooth gray sides, while the others gathered around.

"Let's try to solve this step-by-step," said Holly. "We have to take Silver up to the surface to get some air. But we can't do that, because she's stuck in the net. So, instead of Silver going up to the air . . ."

". . . the air must come down to Silver," shouted Sophie. "Holly, you're a genius!"

"But what do you mean?" asked Scarlett. "We can't bring air down under

the water. It's not something we can carry in our pouches."

"No," said Sophie, "but we can carry it in our mouths, don't you see?"

"Oh!" said Misty. "I understand it now. We mermaids can breathe in the water, and up above in the air. So we'll go up to the surface, take in a nice big breath . . ."

". . . hold it in our mouths . . . ," said Holly.

". . . and breathe it into Silver's blowhole!" finished Sophie triumphantly. She looked around, flushed and eager.

"It sounds very clever," said Lucy. "Do you really think it will work?"

"We won't know until we try," Holly replied. "Smudge, we're going to see if we can breathe for your mommy."

Sophie and Holly sped away up to the surface. They made sure that there were no boats nearby, then bobbed up through the waves to the overwater world. They took in huge gulps of air, closed their mouths, and dived back down to Silver. Then the mermaids took turns to breathe the air gently into her blowhole.

"That's better, Sisters of the Sea," Silver sighed gratefully. "I feel a little stronger now."

"Kind mermaids!" cried Smudge. "Smart mermaids!"

"It seems to be working," said Sophie. "But we have to continue doing it. Scarlett and Misty, why don't you go to the surface next? Bring down some big breaths of air for Silver."

Soon all the mermaids had gotten the hang of it. They went up to the surface and dived back down over and over again, so that Silver could be given the air she needed.

"Thank you," said the patient mother. "But you can't do this forever. How am I going to get out of here? Smudge and I must rejoin our dolphin family before they swim away to the Wild Waves."

"We don't want to be left behind," said little Smudge.

The mermaids' task was only half done. They could help Silver to breathe, but she still couldn't move. What would Sophie and her friends be able to think of next?

Chapter Four

"Where do you think the rest of the dolphins will be now, Silver?" asked Sophie.

All the mermaids knew that it was very important for Silver and Smudge to be reunited with their family. These friendly sea creatures stayed safe by traveling in groups.

"They could be far away," said Silver unhappily. "If you can release me from these ropes we must try to join them soon.

We won't be able to manage the journey to the Wild Waves on our own."

Both she and Smudge looked very worried. The mermaids thought about how much they missed their own families far away in Coral Kingdom. And now Mantora's selfish cruelty had not only trapped Silver, but delayed their journey home with the crystals once more. Yet the kind young friends knew they couldn't leave the helpless mother alone.

"We'll help you to find your family somehow, Silver," exclaimed Sophie. Her friends nodded in agreement.

"What's the best thing to do?" asked Lucy.

"Perhaps now that Silver is feeling stronger, she can send a message to her sisters," replied Holly, who was already

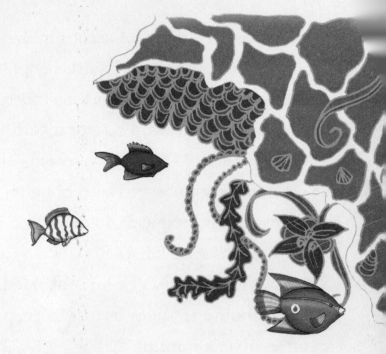

working out an idea in her head. She knew that dolphins were very good at calling to each other under the water. "Do you think you could do that, Silver?"

"I can try," Silver replied slowly. "But even if they hear me and turn back, they won't be able to undo these ropes."

"No, but we've got lots of friends in the sea who might be able to help," smiled Sophie. "The important thing is to find the other dolphins before they swim too far away."

"And don't forget," said Holly wisely, "that some of us must stay here to keep bringing air to Silver. I'd be happy to do that."

"So would I," said Lucy.

"That's settled then," Holly continued. "So who is going to swim as fast as they can after Silver's family?"

Misty, Ellie, and Lucy looked at each other. They knew who was the strongest swimmer! But would Scarlett agree?

"Er . . . perhaps . . . ," Misty began. But Scarlett interrupted her. "Sophie should go to find the dolphins," she said firmly. "She's definitely the fastest swimmer."

Sophie was pleased and surprised. She had never expected Scarlett to say that. But their adventures with the crystals seemed to be bringing out the best in all the mermaids.

"Thank you," she said. "But I don't think I should go alone. What if I get injured or lost? You're a great swimmer too, Scarlett. Will you come with me?"

Now it was Scarlett's turn to look pleased.

"Of course I will," she said happily.

"So that leaves Misty and Ellie," said Holly.

"We'll go and find something sharp to cut

these horrible ropes," said Misty. "Then
Silver and Smudge will be able to leave
with the other dolphins when Sophie
and Scarlett find them."

"Excellent," said Holly. "Now
everyone's got a job to do. Let's get
to work as a team!"

Misty and Ellie quickly said good-bye to
their friends, then kissed the little dolphin.

"We'll be back soon, Smudge," they said,
"with something to free your mommy."

"But hurry!" warned
Holly. "We must be
quick."

"We will,"
replied Misty and
Ellie. With a twirl
of their pink and

purple tails they turned and sped away.
Then Holly and Lucy dashed to the
surface to bring down more gulps of air
for Silver. The mother dolphin explained
weakly where the mermaids might find
her family.

"Thank you, Silver," said Sophie, "we'll
do our very best to catch up with your
sisters."

"Good luck," said Holly.

"And don't be too long!" added Lucy.

Sophie and Scarlett flicked their bright tails and cried, *"Mermaid S.O.S.!"*

They streamed away in the direction that Silver had described, darting around the far edge of the net. This was a race that the mermaids couldn't lose.

The two young friends were perfectly matched as they surged along. Sparkling bubbles swirled around them. Families of surprised fish looked up in wonder as they flashed past. On and on they went, farther and farther, until their arms and tails began to ache.

"Wait!" called Sophie. "Let's just rest for a moment. We've done well so far."

The mermaids could sense that they were moving into deeper waters, and

that the dangerous gill net was now far behind them. The light was dim, and ghostly shapes seemed to sway in the depths below them. Sophie, who wasn't usually afraid of anything, felt a little nervous. She wondered what unknown dangers lay all around them. Mantora could even be lurking nearby, hoping to catch an unwary mermaid in a trap of her own.

"Maybe we should get our crystals out," she whispered to Scarlett.

"Listen!" Scarlett replied, suddenly clutching Sophie's hand. "What's that?"

An eerie, beautiful sound echoed through the sea behind them. It came from where they had left their friends by the sinister gill net.

"It's Silver calling to her family!" cried
Sophie in relief. The mermaids strained to

hear any reply coming from the deep water ahead, but everything was silent.

"I hope they hear her soon," said Scarlett. "If the other dolphin mothers do send messages back to Silver, we will hear their calls, too. That will make it easier for us to find them."

"We *have to* find them," said Sophie. "We can't let Silver down—or her poor little Smudge. Come on!"

Sophie and Scarlett leaped through the sea again, their orange and red tails shimmering like flames as they raced along.

Faster and faster they went, swimming in powerful harmony. Never before had they swum so swiftly and surely.

At last, the tireless young mermaids were rewarded with a wonderful sound. Unmistakable echoing calls reached them from the surface overhead.

"It's the other dolphins," said Sophie. "Oh, Scarlett, we've found them at last!"

Chapter Five

Sophie and Scarlett sped up to the surface through a haze of shimmering bubbles.

"Wait!" said Sophie. "I'll look above the waves first. If we're near any human boats or harbors, I'll dive back down right away to warn you."

Slowly and carefully, she peeped above the surface of the water. A splendid sight met her eyes. A group of dolphins was

leaping through the waves. They were
mothers with their young, just like Silver
and Smudge. As the dolphins dived into the
sea, the spray glittered gold in the sunlight.

Sophie flicked her tail and plunged
down toward Scarlett.

"It's all right!" she said excitedly. "It's
safe to come up."

Scarlett gasped in admiration when
she saw the sleek, silvery dolphins.

"Oh, they're wonderful," she cried.

"But we must speak to them as fast as we can."

"Hi, there!" Sophie called, waving her hands frantically over her head, as she tried to catch their attention.

"Hello, Dolphins," shouted Scarlett. "We've found your friends!"

But the wind and spray seemed to blow the mermaids' voices away. The busy creatures didn't see or hear them.

"They aren't listening," Scarlett groaned. "What can we do? We'll never catch up with them again if they swim too far from us."

"Don't worry," replied Sophie. "I've got an idea."

She quickly opened her glistening orange pouch and took out a small conch shell from her S.O.S. Kit. The shell was marked

all over with colored speckles. Sophie held
it to her lips, took a deep breath, and blew.

A powerful note sounded across the
waves like a warning cry. It was a
Mermaid Call for times of emergency.
Every sea creature who heard it had to

stop and listen. The dolphins stayed still for a moment. They lifted their sleek, friendly faces above the water, looking to see who had made the urgent noise.

"Now take out your crystal, Scarlett!" exclaimed Sophie. "That's right. Hold it up to the sun like this."

Sophie held her pure, sparkling crystal high over her head. The sun's rays struck it and were reflected back over the sea like white flames. Scarlett did the same. The

blazing light caught the attention of the dolphins. Slowly, they began to swim in a circle around the mermaids. The babies kept close to their mothers' sides. Then, one of the mothers spoke. She looked a lot like Silver.

"Greetings, Mermaids!" she said, in a clear voice. "My name is Serena. You have summoned us with your Mermaid Music and the light of the great sun. Tell us what you have to say. We cannot stay long."

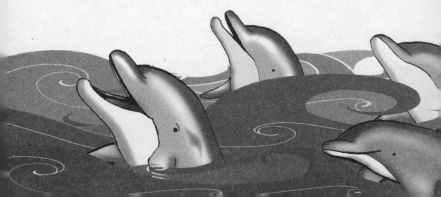

"We think we might be able to help you," said Scarlett eagerly.

"We have found Silver and Smudge," added Sophie.

A ripple of astonishment went through the circle of dolphins.

"You have found our sister and her little one!" said Serena. "We have been searching and calling for them. We thought we heard Silver's call just now, but it was very faint."

"It really was her," replied Sophie. "And we know where she is. She is trapped in a massive gill net. The humans are using it for fishing."

Serena shivered. "So many of us have been harmed by these fearful nets. There is no hope for Silver if she is caught in one." She bowed her head.

"But there is hope!" said Sophie. "Our friends are helping her to breathe. They are going to untie her somehow. But even when Silver is free she can't be left behind. She will be weak after her ordeal. What will happen to Smudge without the whole dolphin family to protect him? It is much safer for them to travel with the rest of you."

The dolphins called softly to each other in their own language. Then Serena turned again to Sophie and Scarlett.

"If what you say is true," she said, "then you bring happy news. But we are all swimming to meet the father dolphins at our summer home in the Wild Waves. We cannot delay too long, or the winds and tides will turn against us."

"We do understand that," said Sophie. "We're in the middle of an important journey too. Queen Neptuna is anxiously

expecting us to return to Coral Kingdom any day now. But sometimes, even an important task has to wait. We have interrupted our journey to help Silver. Will you do the same?"

"You have spoken well," said Serena. "We will trust you and halt our journey for a little while. By coming with you we risk being stranded far from our dear husbands. But Silver is very precious to us. We will take this risk. Lead us to her— and to little Smudge!"

Chapter Six

The journey back to the gill net took nearly all Sophie's and Scarlett's strength. They were already tired from the race to catch up with Silver's family, but somehow they had to find enough energy to return. The dolphins, even the young ones, streaked through the water like silver arrows, and the weary mermaids had to work hard to keep up.

"I don't think I can do it," gasped Scarlett. "I'm so tired!"

"Yes, you can, Scarlett," urged Sophie. "Hold my hand! I'll help you."

So the friends traveled hand in hand and gave each other strength.

At last they arrived at the place where they had left Silver. The other dolphins followed close behind them.

"We're back!" called Sophie breathlessly. "Have you managed to free her?"

But she was very disappointed to see that Silver was still lying helplessly in the tangled ropes. Lucy was taking care of Smudge while Holly breathed gently into Silver's blowhole.

"Misty and Ellie aren't here yet," said Holly quickly. "We're still waiting for them. But you've found Silver's family!"

Silver looked up, her eyes glowing with delight.

"Serena!" she cried. "You came back for us."

"We could not leave you here, my sister,"

replied Serena. "But how are these mermaids going to free you, as they promised?"

Just at that moment, Misty darted into view. She was followed by a comical-looking parade of purply-blue lobsters.

"Misty!" said Sophie. "Have you found a way of cutting the net?"

"I hope so," she replied, with a flourish

of her pink tail. "Do you remember the lobsters we passed on our way? They've come to help. Their armor-plated claws might be strong enough to snap the ropes in two."

The friendly lobsters set to work right away, pinching and pulling the tight ropes with their sharp pincers. Little by little they began to split and fray. Silver managed to ease herself around slightly in the tangled net.

"Keep going," the mermaids shouted in encouragement. "You've almost got it!"

Then Ellie dived down from the surface, rippling her purple tail as she sped off to speak to Silver.

"More help is coming," she told the gentle mother eagerly. "I went up to the surface to call the seabird cry that the albatross taught me. It summoned some passing shearwaters. They will dive into the water and peck the ropes for you with their long beaks."

The lobsters moved out of the way and watched with the astonished dolphins. Eight, nine, ten shearwaters plummeted into the water, pecked at the fraying ropes, then shot back to the surface for air. They were strong, clever birds. Again and again they dived, until Sophie cried, "The ropes have broken. Silver is free!"

"Mommy, mommy," cried Smudge. "You can swim again!"

The mermaids helped to pull away the last bits of net from Silver's gleaming sides. Their team effort had worked—with the

help of the other sea creatures. Sophie and her friends thanked the lobsters gratefully.

"Happy to help," they replied cheerfully. Then they waddled clumsily back to their homes for a rest after their splendid efforts.

Silver's dolphin family filled the sea with their happy, echoing songs, as she swam

slowly toward the surface. Little Smudge
followed very close behind.

"Oh, it is wonderful to breathe in the air
again," Silver sighed weakly. She had
reached the sunlit waves at last. "It is so
good to be free."

The shearwaters hovered gracefully
above the water.

"Thank you," called Ellie. "Fly free and
safely!"

"We will," they cried.

The mermaids waved and
watched the seabirds
flap their wings and
whirl away.

"How lucky we are
to have you back with
us," said Serena, as the

dolphins nuzzled their beaks against Silver
and Smudge. "Now we will travel safely as
a family all the way to the Wild Waves.
How can we thank you, Sisters of the Sea?"

"We don't need thanks," said Lucy
shyly. "We're just glad that you are all
together again."

"And now we must be traveling on, too,
as fast as we can," said Holly.

The young friends knew that Holly was
right. If they didn't get home in time with

the crystals, then Coral Kingdom would b
destroyed. They couldn't bear to think of
Mantora setting up her evil Storm
Kingdom and ruling the seas in Queen
Neptuna's place, with fear instead of love.

"Yes, we must go," Sophie agreed.
"Queen Neptuna is waiting for us and the
crystals."

"Ooh, crystals! Can we see them?" asked
Smudge.

"Of course," smiled Sophie. "Just for a
minute."

The mermaids quickly drew the crystals
from their pouches. They held them out on
the palms of their hands, so that Smudge
and the other dolphins could see their
beauty. As the sun glinted on the magic
stones, a dazzling arc of light suddenly

not out from them and poured over Silver.
She looked as though she had been
crowned in warm, golden sunshine.

"I can feel all my strength returning,"
she exclaimed. "Your crystals have cured
me. Now I am ready for our long journey!"

"And we really must begin our journey again," said the mermaids. "It's time to say farewell."

"Why don't you swim with us?" begged Silver and Serena. "We are going in your direction for a while. It will be one last race for you."

"Pretty mermaids, swim with us!" said Smudge.

Sophie and Scarlett looked at each other and laughed.

"One last race?" said Sophie, with a grin.

"One last race," smiled Scarlett. "Let's make a splash together!"

The mermaids hid the gleaming crystals in their pouches. Then they set off joyfully with their dolphin friends, speeding through the water. Their tails glistened

orange, purple, red, green, pink, and
yellow in the sparkling waves.

On and on the mermaids raced, their
hearts proud and brave, longing to reach
their home once more. Sophie and her
friends felt that nothing could stop them
from returning to Coral Kingdom now.

But as the steadfast young mermaids

continued on their way, Mantora was already scheming to spoil their hopes and dreams. She had plenty of trouble brewing for the Sisters of the Sea!

Read all the books in the Mermaid S.O.S. series!

Misty to the Rescue
gillian shields

Ellie and the Secret Potion
gillian shields

Sophie Makes a Splash
gillian shields

Holly Takes a Risk
gillian shields

Scarlett's New Friend
gillian shields

Lucy and the Magic Crystal
gillian shields